Bingo Lingo

Supporting **literacy** with songs and rhymes

by Helen MacGregor

with additional material by Kaye Umansky
and with illustrations by Michael Evans
Literacy consultant: Lynn Mills

A & C Black · London

Contents

Introduction

1. **Hello around the world**
   greetings in other languages

Playing with sounds

2. **Jamaquacks**
   inventing and copying
3. **Some names**
   exploring names
4. **Old MacGregor had a zoo**
   developing awareness of sounds
5. **Mashed potato**
   patterns of sounds
6. **Chatterbox**
   patterns of sounds
7. **My machine**
   patterns of sounds
8. **Sleeping Beauty**
   patterns of sounds; sequencing
9. **Storm**
   patterns of sounds; -sh endings

Rhyme

10. **Yoyo**
    exploring rhyme
11. **Grandma and the flea**
    experiencing rhyme
12. **Captain of the aeroplane**
    experiencing rhyme
13. **Whatever the weather**
    experiencing rhyme; sequencing
14. **Whoops!**
    predicting rhymes; number sequence
15. **Hey, little playmate (1st version)**
    experiencing rhyme; sequencing
16. **Hey, little playmate (2nd version)**
    predicting rhymes; sequencing
17. **No room**
    generating rhymes; sequencing
18. **A plate of potatoes**
    generating rhymes
19. **Little red jeep**
    generating rhymes; listening skills

Onset and rime

20. **When I feel sad**
    extending sound play; listening skills; onset
21. **Seaside song**
    -ee
22. **Spooky song**
    -oo
23. **The hungry rabbit**
    -op; sequencing
24. **Old MacGregor's holiday**
    blends featuring l; -ip, -op endings
25. **The bat and cat**
    CVC words; short and long vowels

Alphabet and letters

- 26 **Animals' alphabet rap**
  alliteration; sequencing
- 27 **Alphabet's tea**
  sequence
- 28 **What shall we do?**
  finding letters in words
- 29 **Letter shapes**
  writing letter shapes
- 30 **Teatime treats**
  alliteration
- 31 **'Magic e'**
  'magic e' (split vowel digraph); spelling
- 32 **Bingo lingo**
  identifying initial phonemes; spelling
- 33 **Baby's bed**
  reading and spelling common CVC words

Word endings

- 34 **The wishing well**
  -ll
- 35 **Quick, duck, quack**
  -ck
- 36 **Huff puff**
  -ff
- 37 **Party time**
  -ss
- 38 **Sing-song**
  -ng

Grammar

- 39 **Yes, no**
  questions and answers
- 40 **What's she doing?**
  questions and answers; verbs
- 41 **This old lady**
  verbs; number sequence
- 42 **My hat**
  adjectives
- 43 **Opposites**
  antonyms

Time to go home

- 44 **What did we read?**
  reviewing

Song melodies

First lines index

Introduction

Second edition 2005
Reprinted 2006
A&C Black Publishers Ltd
38 Soho Square
London W1D 3HB
First published 1999 © 1999, 2005

ISBN 10: 0 7136 7324 9
ISBN 13: 978 0 7136 7324 1

All rights reserved. No part of this publication (except for the photocopiable material indicated with songs 14, 22, 23, 27 and 33) may be reproduced or used in any form or by any means – photographic, electronic or mechanical, including photocopying, recording, taping or information storage and retrieval systems – without the prior permission in writing of the publishers.

Text © 2005, 1999 Helen MacGregor
Additional songs and rhymes: © 1999 Kaye Umansky
Literacy consultant: Lynn Mills
Illustrations © 1999 Michael Evans
Cover artwork © 1999 Alex Ayliffe
Editor: Ana Sanderson, Marie Penny
Cover design: Peter Bailey
Text Design: Carla Moss
Illustrator: Michael Evans
Cover illustration: Alex Ayliffe

Printed in Great Britain by
St Edmundsbury Press,
Bury St Edmunds, Suffolk.

A&C Black uses paper produced with elemental chlorine-free pulp, harvested from managed sustainable forests.

From infancy, children gain great pleasure from the songs, rhymes and rhythms which help them to remember words and develop good listening skills. **Bingo Lingo** is a resource full of material that will capture children's imaginations. It was written and compiled for that exciting stage in a child's development when (s)he begins to develop sound (phonological) awareness and experience the spoken language system upon which the development of literacy relies.

Playing with sounds

These activities encourage children to explore vocal sounds: remembering and copying; inventing their own; and investigating patterns of sound through songs and chants. There are many opportunities for links with writing, eg the animal sounds suggested by the children for *Old MacGregor had a zoo* can be made into a frieze by the children or scribed by the teacher as appropriate.

Rhyme

In this section, the focus is on rhyme, through which children learn to categorise words by sound, increasing their potential to read and write. Experience of rhyming words later leads to comparisons of different spellings of the same sounds. The musical games and songs in this section build a child's memory for the pitch, tone and intensity of language as well as providing a fun way of improving phonological awareness. The songs here give children experience of rhymes and also opportunities for predicting and making their own rhyming phrases. Rhyme also draws attention to the two very important language units: onset and rime.

Onset and rime

There are three levels of phonological awareness: syllables; onset and rime; and phonemes (a sound in a word). Children need to be able to break words into syllables before they can break them into phonemes, and they naturally find it much simpler to break up words into 'onsets' and 'rimes' than into single phonemes (*b-est* rather than *b-e-s-t*; *w-in/d-ow* rather than *w-i-n-d-o-w*). The songs here are based on changing onsets which reinforce the child's understanding of these two elements, as in *Spooky song's h-oo, b-oo, sh-oo, wh-oo*. Songs in this section can also be used to develop the key skill of blending phonemes into words for reading. Consonant Vowel Consonant (CVC) words feature in both this and the following section and can be used to develop reading and spelling.

Alphabet and letters; word endings; grammar

The last three sections of the book provide musical activities with more specific teaching points, including the use of 'magic e', word endings, adjectives and opposites (antonyms). Many of these can be used with children whose literacy skills are more advanced and they also provide further opportunities for reading and writing.

Teachers' notes

The following symbols are used in the teachers' notes:

 indicates a basic description of the activity;

 gives ideas for further literacy development with questions, investigations or extensions;

 indicates a musical activity.

A summary of the literacy focus of each song, rhyme or rap can be found at the top of the teachers' notes boxes.

The first melody notes of each tune are indicated at the bottom of the corresponding Teachers' notes box. If any tune is unknown to you, you will find it written out at the back of the book, together with the new words. If you don't read music, find someone who does to teach the songs to you. If you know a different version of a tune from the one we have given, do use it as the new words will still fit.

The songs in **Bingo Lingo** are simple to incorporate into daily classroom routines. They enable a multi-sensory approach to literacy work which is necessary to compensate for weaknesses, while building on strengths. Let the essential elements of active participation and fun enhance the learning of your children!

Helen MacGregor and Lynn Mills

Acknowledgements

All the songs and rhymes in this collection were written by Helen MacGregor, except for the following by Kaye Umansky:
12 Captain of the aeroplane, 13 Whatever the weather, 17 No room, 18 A plate of potatoes, 19 Little red jeep, 27 Alphabet's tea, 34 The wishing well, 35 Quick, duck, quack, 36 Huff, puff, and 37 Party time; © 1999 Kaye Umansky.
3 Some names is an adaptation of the song Some sounds are short by Sue Nicholls, in Bobby Shaftoe, clap your hands, published by A&C Black.

The author and publishers would like to thank the following people for their generous help during the preparation of this book: Jon Appleton, Paul Gregory, Harriet Lowe, Marion Lang, Alasdair MacGregor, Audrey Mason, Sue Nicholls, Linda Read, Sheena Roberts and Jane Sebba.

① Hello around the world

Tune: **If you're happy and you know it**

Solo:	All (chant):
When you want to say *hello* around the world,	*Hello!*
When you want to say *hello* around the world,	*Hello!*
When you want to say *hello*,	
Sing this song and you will know	
How to greet your friends from all around the world.	*Hello!*
When you greet your friends in *French* you say *bonjour,*	*Bonjour!*
When you greet your friends in *French* you say *bonjour,*	*Bonjour!*
When you want to say *hello*,	
Sing this song and you will know	
When you greet your friends in *French* you say *bonjour.*	*Bonjour!*
When you greet your friends in *Hindi* you say *namusti* ...	*Namusti!*
When you greet your friends in *Italian* you say *ciao* ...	*Ciao!*

FOCUS   greetings in other languages

 This song is a useful starting point for collecting and comparing greetings from different cultures. Continue adding more verses using languages relevant to the children. Here are some additional examples together with pronunciation guides: *Swahili: jambo (jamboh); Spanish: hola (ohla); Mandarin: hi (high); Yoruba: bawoni (bawohnee).*

C	C F	F F	F F	F E	F G
When	you want	to say	hel - lo	a - round	the world

Playing with sounds

Jamaquacks
Circle game

Jamaquack, jamaquack, jamaquack jive,
Jamaquacks sing when the clock strikes five.
One, two, three, four, five.

   Sam: *zeeeeeeee*
   All: *zeeeeeeee*

Jamaquack, jamaquack, jamaquack jive,
Jamaquacks sing when the clock strikes five.
One, two, three, four, five.

   Kate: *lee li lee li lo*
   All: *lee li lee li lo*

Jamaquack, jamaquack, jamaquack jive...

> **Focus** inventing and copying
>
> ★ This circle game encourages children to invent, memorise and copy vocal sounds. Jamaquacks are imaginary creatures who speak a made-up language. The children sit in a circle and pass a toy microphone around as they say the chant together. Whoever is holding the microphone on number five makes up a jamaquack word or phrase. The rest of the children copy it and the game continues.

Some names
Tune: Pease pudding hot

Some names are short,
Some names are long.
Please tell us your name
After this song.

> **Focus** exploring names
>
> ★ Explore children's names. Find similarities, eg those which begin with the same letter or sound, or have the same number of syllables.

D	D	E	F#
Some	names	are	short

Old MacGregor had a zoo

Tune: Old MacDonald had a farm

Old MacGregor had a zoo, ee i ee i o.
And in that zoo she had some *snakes*, ee i ee i o.
  With a ssss ssss here and a ssss ssss there,
  Here a ssss, there a ssss, everywhere a ssss ssss,
Old MacGregor had a zoo, ee i ee i o.

... *hippos ... grum grum ...*

... *parrots ... hello hello ...*

Playing with sounds

Focus developing awareness of sounds

 Explore letter sounds, made-up words, through to whole words in this version of the old favourite. The children make up new verses by choosing their own selection of animals and their sounds.

Make a frieze illustrating the animals and the sounds the children have suggested. Use this to investigate letter sounds and digraphs (two letters giving one sound), made-up words, and whole words.

G	G	G	D	E	E	D
Old	Mac-	Gre-	gor	had	a	zoo

5. Mashed potato

Chant

Scrub-a-dub, scrub-a-dub,
Chip-chop, chip-chop,
Hubble-bubble, hubble-bubble,
Mish-mash, mish-mash,
Mmmmmmmmmmm.

> Focus patterns of sounds
>
> Perform this chant with rhythmic hand actions for each line.
>
> Perform it as a round.

6. Chatterbox

Tune: Pat-a-cake

Chatterbox, chatterbox chats all day,
Chatterbox can't hear what I want to say.
Chattering, nattering, yackety-yack,
Chatterbox, chatterbox, let me talk back!

Chanted word patterns:
1. *Yac-ke-ty, yac-ke-ty yac-ke-ty yack* (x4)
2. *Clac-ke-ty clack, clac-ke-ty clack* (x4)
3. *Jab-ber and blab-ber, jab-ber and blab-ber* (x4)

> Focus patterns of sounds
>
> Alternate singing the song with chanting each word pattern four times.
>
> Divide the children into three groups to chant the word patterns at the same time to make a chattering effect.
>
> Suggest more word patterns, eg *chatter, natter; mumble, grumble.*
>
> C E G C E G
> Chat- ter- box, chat- ter- box

7 My machine

Tune: The wheels on the bus

Today I made a fine machine,
Fine machine, fine machine,
Today I made a fine machine,
Can you hear?

The cogs have teeth on my machine,
My machine, my machine,
The cogs have teeth on my machine,
Can you hear?
  Chant: *Trick-track, trick-track, trick-track, trick-track* (x4)

The wheels spin round on my machine,
My machine, my machine,
The wheels spin round on my machine,
Can you hear?
  Chant: *Zoop, zoop, zoop, zoop* (x4)

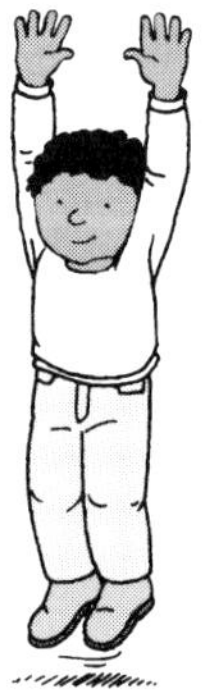

Springs coil and stretch on my machine …
  Chant: *Boing, shhhhhhhhhh* (x4)

The levers move on my machine …
  Chant: *Um-chicky-um-pah, um-chicky-um-pah* (x4)

Playing with sounds

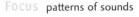 Playing with sounds

The whistle blows on my machine ...
    Chant: *Beebeeeeeeeeep,   beebeeeeeeeeep* (x4)

Today I made a fine machine,
Fine machine, fine machine,
Today I made a fine machine,
Can you hear?
    Chant: *Trick-track, trick-track, trick-track, trick-track ...*
          Zoop,   zoop,   zoop,   zoop ...
          Boing,   shhhhhhhhhh ...
          Um-chicky-um-pah, um-chicky-um-pah ...
          Beebeeeeeeeep,   beebeeeeeeeeep ...

Focus   patterns of sounds

 Teach this song one verse at a time, comparing the chanted sound effects at the end of each verse. Ask the children to contribute different ways of using their voices to say each sound, eg making voices swoop from low to high on *zoop*.

 Divide the children into five groups to perform the chants one at a time. Can each group perform its chant independently? (You may need to tap a steady beat to prevent the performances from speeding up.)

 Combine all five chants. Choose a conductor who signals to each group in turn to begin until all five are chanting simultaneously. The groups repeat their chants until the conductor signals either to stop or to perform an ending. (Perhaps the machine can get louder and louder until it blows up with a loud bang and a hiss!)

 In small groups, individual children can invent new chanted sound effects. Then together they can build a machine by combining the chants after the last verse. They may like to find ways of writing down their sounds pictorially or in letters.

C	F	F	F A	C'	A	F
To-	day	I	made a	fine	ma-	chine

8 Sleeping Beauty

Rap

The beginning (a very long time ago)

	Let's tell the	**sto**-ry of	**Sleep**-ing	**Beau**-ty.
	Are you	**rea**-dy?	**Once** upon a	**time** –
– there was a	**ba**-by,	*Goo,*	*goo* *ga*	*goo,*
Her name was	**Ro**-sa;	*Goo,*	*goo* *ga*	*goo,*
The fairies	**saw** her,	*Fly,*	*flee* *fly*	*flo,*
And made good	**wi**-shes.	*Fly,*	*flee* *fly*	*flo,*
But then a	**wi**-cked witch	*Ha,*	*ha* *hee*	*ha,*
Waved her	**ma**-gic wand,	*Ha,*	*ha* *hee*	*ha,*
'Be careful,	**Prin**-cess,	*Whoa,*	*whoa* *whoa*	*whoa,*
Keep clear of	**spin**-ning wheels.'	*Whoa,*	*whoa* *whoa*	*whoa.*

The middle (eighteen years later)

The princess	**grew** up	*Grow,*	*grow* *grow*	*grow,*
From one to	**eigh**-teen,	*Grow,*	*grow* *grow*	*grow,*
And then di-	**sas**-ter,	*No,*	*no* *no*	*no,*
She found a	**spin**-ning wheel.	*No,*	*no* *no*	*no,*
She pricked her	**fin**-ger,	*Ow,*	*ow* *ee*	*oh,*
Which made the	**spell** work;	*Ow,*	*ow* *ee*	*oh,*
And she fell a-	**sleep**	*Sh,*	*sh* *sh*	*sh,*
For one hundred	**years**.	*Sh,*	*sh* *sh*	*sh.*

Playing with sounds

Playing with sounds

The end (a century later)

A prince came **rid**-ing	**clop**	**clop**	*clip*	*clop,*
Up to the **cas**-tle;	**clop**	**clop**	*clip*	*clop,*
He started **chop**-ping	**chop**	**chop**	*chip*	*chop,*
Through all the **bram**-bles.	**chop**	**chop**	*chip*	*chop,*
Then he kissed **Ro**-sa	**kiss**	**kiss**	*kiss*	*kiss,*
To break the **bad** spell.	**kiss**	**kiss**	*kiss*	*kiss,*
And they were **mar**-ried	**ding**	**ding**	*dong*	*ding,*
To sounds of **wed**-ding bells;	**ding**	**ding**	*dong*	*ding,*
And they **lived**	**ding**	**ding**	*dong*	*ding,*
Very **hap**-pily	**ding**	**ding**	*dong*	*ding.*
Ever **af**-ter!				

Focus   patterns of sounds; sequencing

   Perform the rap at a steady tempo, clapping or tapping a steady beat throughout. The clapped beats are shown by the syllables set in bold.

   Introduce the rap to the children by performing it all the way through. Encourage the children to join in with the sound patterns (given in italics). They can make up actions to go with them. Younger children will enjoy making the sound patterns and actions after you say each line, while older children will enjoy learning the whole rap.

   Choose another story the children know well and ask them to re-tell it, sequencing short phrases which alternate with simple sound patterns, eg *Once upon a time, doo, doo bee doo, there was a little red hen, cluck, cluck cluck cluck …* You can scribe a piece of shared writing for the whole class as or work with small groups.

9 Storm

Vocal sound picture

Hush   hush
Splish   splash   splish   splash
Rush   dash   rush   dash
Splish   splash   splish   splash
Slish   slosh   slish   slosh
Splish   splash   splish   splash
Bash   lash   bash   lash
Splish   splash   splish   splash
Crash   flash
Splish   splash   splish   splash
Bash   lash   bash   lash
Splish   splash   splish   splash
Slish   slosh   slish   slosh
Splish   splash   splish   splash
Rush   dash   rush   dash
Splish   splash   splish   splash
Hush   hush
Splish   splash   splish   splash
Wishhhhhhhhhhhhhhhhhhhhhhhhhhhhhhhhh............

 Focus patterns of sounds; –sh endings

★ This evocation of a storm in vocal sounds – a sound picture – begins quietly, gets louder, then quieter again. Teach it by asking the children to say just the *splish splash splish splash* lines at first. They should follow your rise and fall in volume as you say the alternate lines. Gradually teach them all the words.

 Perform the sound picture in two groups, alternating lines.

 Perform the sound picture with one group of children repeating *splish splash* throughout, (as an ostinato), while a second group says the whole poem.

 The children can make other vocal sound pictures by choosing and repeating collections of sounds and words, eg *hweee, pop, ooeeeooo* ... for a sound picture of a fairground.

Yoyo

Tune: Oranges and lemons

Once I had a yoyo,
But my yoyo wouldn't go go.
My friend Flo said, 'No no!
That is not the way to yoyo.

You roll it to the top top,
And then you let it drop drop.
When it climbs the string,
You don't do a thing.

Then give a little flick flick,
Now you've nearly learnt the trick trick.'
But when I tried to yoyo,
It still wouldn't go go.

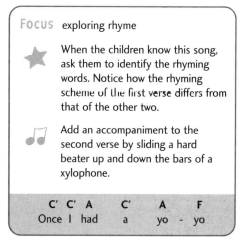

Focus exploring rhyme

- When the children know this song, ask them to identify the rhyming words. Notice how the rhyming scheme of the first verse differs from that of the other two.
- Add an accompaniment to the second verse by sliding a hard beater up and down the bars of a xylophone.

C'	C'	A	C'	A	F
Once	I	had	a	yo	- yo

11 Grandma and the flea

Tune: A sailor went to sea

My Grandma found a flea, flea, flea,
A-swimming in her tea, tea, tea.
She took a spoon and fished it out,
And gave the flea to me, me, me.

I made the flea a bed, bed, bed,
To rest his little head, head, head.
But when I went to say, 'Good night,'
Well, this is what he said, said, said:

'I do not want to nap, nap, nap,
I'm not a sleepy chap, chap, chap.
I'd rather dance all through the night,
And make my feet go tap, tap, tap.'

He danced all through the night, night, night,
Until the morning light, light, light.
When I woke up he winked his eye,
And hopped off out of sight, sight, sight.

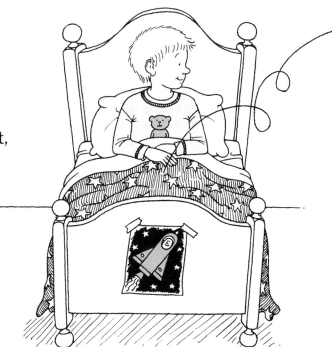

My Grandma, she got up, up, up,
And made some tea to sup, sup, sup.
The flea was doing loop the loops,
And fell into her cup, cup, cup.

My Grandma found a flea, flea, flea ...

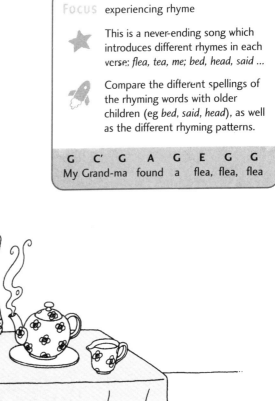

Focus   experiencing rhyme

★ This is a never-ending song which introduces different rhymes in each verse: *flea, tea, me; bed, head, said ...*

🚀 Compare the different spellings of the rhyming words with older children (eg *bed, said, head*), as well as the different rhyming patterns.

G	C'	G	A	G	E	G	G
My	Grand-ma	found	a	flea,	flea,	flea

12 Captain of the aeroplane

Rhyme

Tune: John Brown's body

I'm captain of the aeroplane and this is my salute,
I've got shiny, silver buttons on my special captain's suit.
I climb into my cockpit and I strap myself in tight,
And we're off! Enjoy the flight!

Chorus:
   Can you hear the engines roaring?
   Soon we'll all be up and soaring,
   In the sky we'll go exploring
   Inside my aeroplane.

We rattle down the runway and we really pick up speed,
Then we rise into the heavens which are very high indeed.
We fly around for hours and hours as high as high can be,
And we're back in time for tea.

Chorus:
   Can you hear the engines roaring ...

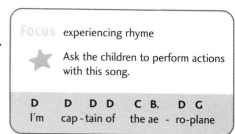

Focus: experiencing rhyme

Ask the children to perform actions with this song.

D	D	D	D	C	B,	D	G
I'm	cap-	tain of		the ae	-	ro-	plane

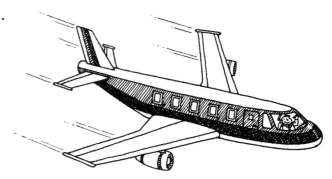

13 Whatever the weather

Rhyme

Chant

Whether the weather is windy,
Whether the weather is grey,
We don't care whatever the weather,
We're going out to play!

Group 1:	Group 2:
Stiff breeze?	Yes, please!
Warm sun?	That'll be fun!
Thick fog?	Take the dog!
Hail storm?	Wrap up warm!
Really hot?	So what!
Cold ice?	That'll be nice!
Hard rain?	Brolly again!
Deep snow?	Cheerio!

Whether the weather is windy,
Whether the weather is grey,
We don't care whatever the weather,
We're going out to play!

 Focus: experiencing rhyme; sequencing

 Teach the children the chorus first, then the verse of weather rhymes one line at a time. To help them memorise the sequence, use eight cards showing symbols representing the different types of weather conditions.

 Divide the children into two groups to perform the verse as shown.

 Point out to older children the use of question marks and exclamation marks, and remind them to vary their intonation when they see them.

 Ask the children to choose instrumental sounds to match each line of the verse, eg *stiff breeze* – shake maracas; *warm sun* – soft beater on a cymbal. Add these sounds to the verse, playing each sound with its matching line.

 Use the picture cards to cue the sequence of instrumental weather sounds as an interlude between speaking the verse and chorus, ie
chorus –
instrumental sounds –
verse etc.

14 Whoops!

Chant

A peanut sat on the railway track,
His heart was all a-flutter,
Round the bend came number one,
Whoops! Peanut *butter*!

A strawberry sat on the railway track,
Her teeth were wobbling loose,
Round the bend came number two,
Whoops! Strawberry *mousse*!

A lemon sat on the railway track,
His eyes were on his belly,
Around the bend came number three,
Whoops! Lemon *jelly*!

An orange sat on the railway track,
Her face required a wash,
Round the bend came number four,
Whoops! Orange *squash*!

A tomato sat on the railway track,
His skin was red, of course,
Around the bend came number five,
Whoops! Tomato *sauce*!

14 Whoops! – *photocopiable pictures*

Rhyme

A potato sat on the railway track,
A smile was on his lips,
Around the bend came number six,
Whoops! Potato *chip*s!

A biscuit sat on the railway track,
A-twiddling her thumbs,
Around the bend came number seven,
Whoops! Biscuit *crumbs*!

Some fruit and nuts sat on the track
Feeling rather sad,
A hungry traveller took them home,
Which wasn't quite so *bad*!
Or was it?

14 Whoops! – *photocopiable pictures*

> Focus predicting rhymes; number sequence
>
>   Teach the first two verses to the children, then say each following verse, omitting the final word (shown in italics). Ask the children to supply the rhyming word for each verse.
>
>   Use the photocopiable picture to remind the children of the seqence of verses. Can they take a train journey backwards along the track and reverse the sequence using the picture cues?
>
>   Ask a small group of children to accompany the chant with vocal train sounds, eg *choo choo choo choo* or *click clack click clack*.

15. Hey, little playmate (1st version)

Tune: Hush little baby

Hey, little playmate, don't you cry,
I'm going to sing you a lullaby.

If that lullaby sounds too loud,
I'm going to buy you a little cloud.

If that little cloud starts to rain,
I'm going to buy you a railway train.

If that railway train leaves too soon,
I'm going to buy you a big balloon.

If that big balloon then goes pop,
I'm going to buy you a spinning top.

If that spinning top spins too fast,
The next gift I buy will be the last!

Rhyme

Focus: experiencing rhyme; sequencing

 Teach this new version of the traditional song to give experience of rhyming patterns.

D	B	B	B	C'	B	A	A
Hey,	lit-	tle play-	mate,	don't	you		cry

16 Hey, little playmate (2nd version)

Tune: Hush little baby

Hey, little playmate, don't say a thing,
I'm going to buy you a piece of *string*.

If that piece of string's too thick,
I'm going to buy you a baby *chick*.

If that baby chick won't cluck,
I'm going to buy you a plastic *duck*.

If that plastic duck won't float,
I'm going to buy you a sailing *boat*.

If that sailing boat won't go far,
I'm going to buy you a bright red *car*.

If that bright red car won't park,
I'm going to buy you a snapping *shark*.

If that snapping shark won't bite,
I'm going to buy you a big blue *kite*.

If that big blue kite won't fly,
I'm going to buy you an apple *pie*.

If that apple pie tastes funny,
I'm going to buy you a fluffy *bunny*.

If that fluffy bunny runs away,
That will be the last thing I buy *today*!

FOCUS predicting rhymes; sequencing

 In this version of the song, the second rhyming word in each couplet is italicised. Omit it and ask the children to predict it.

 With older children, investigate the different spelling patterns of pairs of rhymes eg
bite, kite – same spelling (rime);
pie, fly – different spellings.

D	B	B	B	C'	B	A	A	A
Hey,	lit-	tle	play-	mate,	don't	say	a	thing

Rhyme

No room
Chant

I get in my bed at bedtime,
It's as crowded as can be.
   I sleep with a doll, I sleep with a troll,
There's hardly room for me!

I get in my bed at bedtime,
It's as crowded as can be.
   I'm into the habit of cuddling rabbit,
   I sleep with a doll, I sleep with a troll,
There's hardly room for me!

   ... I've got to have Ted, right here by my head ...

   ... My armadillo is under the pillow ...

I get in my bed at bedtime,
It's as crowded as can be.
   I need my sheep to help me to sleep,
   My armadillo is under the pillow,
   I've got to have Ted right here, by my head,
   I'm into the habit of cuddling rabbit,
   I sleep with a doll, I sleep with a troll,
There's no room left for me, BUMP!

 Focus generating rhymes; sequencing

This is a cumulative rhyme – it grows as a new toy is added in each verse.

 Use pictures or real toys to help children remember the sequence as each new toy is introduced.

 The children may like to extend the number of toys in the chant by making up new rhymes, eg:
I put my green frog next to my dog;
I find room for panda, her name is Amanda;
I hug crocodile, he makes me smile.

18 A plate of potatoes

Rhyme

Chant

A plate of potatoes, a plate of potatoes,
There's nothing as great
As a plate of potatoes!

1st solo: Baked in foil, fried in oil,
All: There's nothing as great
As a plate of potatoes!

2nd solo: Cooked in a curry, boiled in a hurry,
All: There's nothing as great
As a plate of potatoes!

3rd solo: Stewed in a pot? Give me the lot!
All: There's nothing as great
As a plate of potatoes!

4th solo: Mashed with cheese? Mmm, yes please!
All: There's nothing as great
As a plate of potatoes!

A plate of potatoes, a plate of potatoes,
There's nothing as great
As a plate of potatoes!

Focus generating rhymes

 The lines describing different cooking methods give children experience of rhymes. The chant can be performed by all the children, with four soloists, or groups of children saying the first line of each verse.

 Older children can notice the same spelling patterns (rime) in the first three verses (foil, oil; curry, hurry; pot, lot) and the different spellings in the last verse (cheese, please).

 Ask the children to make more recipe chants using the same structure, eg
A plate of spaghetti ...
Topped with sauce, tomato,
of course ...
Beans on toast ...
Heated through, they're good
for you ...

Rhyme

19 Little red jeep
Chant

Let's go for a drive in the little red jeep,
   Beep, beep! Beep-beep-beep!
Drive up the mountain, tall and steep,
   Beep, beep! Beep-beep-beep!

Over the mountain, down we go,
   Beep, beep! Beep-beep-beep!
On with the brake now, nice and slow,
   Beep, beep! Beep-beep-beep!

Into the town with lots of shops,
   Beep, beep! Beep-beep-beep!
Driving slow, with starts and stops,
   Beep, beep! Beep-beep-beep!

The stars are out, it's time to sleep,
   Beep, beep! Beep-beep-beep!
Say goodnight to the little red jeep,
   Beep, beep! Beep-beep-beep!

Focus	generating rhymes; listening skills
	Ask the children to chant the *beep* pattern after you say the first and third lines of each verse. Then teach them the whole chant.
	Ask the children to make up more verses describing the little red jeep's journey.
	Extend the listening skills of the children by varying the speed of each verse. Can the children copy your tempo with their *beep beep* response?
	Whisper the last verse, asking the children to match your volume.

When I feel sad

Chant

When I feel sad I *hum* a song.
   Ha-ha-hum, ha-ha-hum, ha-ha-ha-ha-hum,
I *hum* a song when it all goes wrong.
   Ha-ha-hum, ha-ha-hum, ha-ha-ha-ha-hum,
I *hum* a song all through the day.
   Ha-ha-hum, ha-ha-hum, ha-ha-ha-ha-hum,
Until that sadness goes away.
   Ha-ha-hum, ha-ha-hum, ha-ha-ha-ha-hum,
   Ha-ha-hum, ha-ha-hum, ha-ha-ha-ha-hum.

When I feel sad I *dum* a song.
   Da-da-dum, da-da-dum, da-da-da-da-dum ...

When I feel sad I *fum* a song.
   Fa-fa-fum, fa-fa-fum, fa-fa-fa-fa-fum ...

Onset and rime

 Focus extending sound play; listening skills; onset

 This chant encourages children to discriminate between similar sounds
eg *ha, da, fa*.

 Teach the chant. Then ask the children to make up new verses,
eg *mum: ma-ma-mum;*
lum: la-la-lum;
glum: gla-gla-glum ...

 When the children know the chant well, play with the sound patterns by altering the speed and rhythm, then ask the children to copy accurately.

 Add percussion instruments to the sound patterns or replace the sound words as you play the rhythm of each sound pattern.

Adapt the song to explore different sounds:
When I get ill, I bong my bell,
Binga-bong, binga-bong, binga-binga-binga-bong;
I bong my bell till I get well,
Binga-bong, binga-bong, binga-binga-binga-bong ...

21 Seaside song

Tune: Skip to my Lou

Giggling baby, *hee, hee, hee,*
Giggling baby, *hee, hee, hee,*
Giggling baby, *hee, hee, hee,*
Hee-hee, hee-hee, my darling.

Chorus: *Hee, hee, hee-hee, hee-hee,*
Hee, hee, hee-hee, hee-hee,
Hee, hee, hee-hee, hee-hee,
Hee-hee, hee-hee, my darling.

Buzzing insect, *zee, zee, zee* ...

Chorus: *Zee, zee, zee-zee, zee-zee* ...

Waves on the seashore, *shee, shee, shee* ...

Chorus: *Shee, shee, shee-shee, shee-shee* ...

Throwing beach-balls, *whee, whee, whee* ...

Chorus: *Whee, whee, whee-whee, whee-whee* ...

Here at the seaside, one, two, three ...
Hee, bee, shee, whee, my darling.

Chorus: *Hee, bee, hee-bee, shee-whee* ...
Hee, bee, shee, whee, my darling.

Onset and rime

> **Focus** -ee
>
> ⭐ Notice the onset (*h, z, sh, wh*) and rime in *Seaside song* (-ee) and opposite in *Spooky song* (-oo). Draw the children's attention to their written forms. Make pictures to illustrate each version of the song, encouraging the children to add the sound words.
>
> Make up new words for the song, choosing different scenes and sound patterns.
>
> Add a different instrumental sound to each -ee or -oo word.
>
> | F# | F# | D | D | F# | F# | A |
> |----|----|---|---|----|----|---|
> | Gig- | gling | ba - | by, | hee, | hee, | hee |

22 Spooky song

Tune: Skip to my Lou

Owl at midnight, *hoo, hoo, hoo,*
Owl at midnight, *hoo, hoo, hoo,*
Owl at midnight, *hoo, hoo, hoo,*
Hoo-hoo, hoo-hoo, so spooky.

Chorus: *Hoo, hoo, hoo-hoo, hoo-hoo,*
Hoo, hoo, hoo-hoo, hoo-hoo,
Hoo, hoo, hoo-hoo, hoo-hoo,
Hoo-hoo, hoo-hoo, so spooky.

> **Focus** -oo
>
> Show the children the photocopiable pictures and ask them to find the -oo sounds hidden in each one.
>
> | F♯ | F♯ | D | D | F♯ | F♯ | A |
> |---|---|---|---|---|---|---|
> | Owl | at | mid- | night, | *hoo,* | *hoo,* | *hoo* |

Hide in the darkness, *boo, boo, boo* ...

Chorus: *Boo, boo, boo-boo, boo-boo* ...

Bats in the belfry, *shoo, shoo, shoo* ...

Chorus: *Shoo, shoo, shoo-shoo, shoo-shoo* ...

Whistling wild wind, *whoo, whoo, whoo* ...

Chorus: *Whoo, whoo, whoo-whoo, whoo-whoo* ...

Don't leave me here, I'll come too ...
Hoo, boo, shoo, whoo, so spooky.

Chorus: *Hoo, boo, hoo-boo, shoo-whoo* ...
Hoo, boo, shoo, whoo, so spooky.

22 Spooky song – *photocopiable pictures*

23 The hungry rabbit

Tune: There was a princess long ago

I saw a hungry rabbit *hop*,
   Hop, hop, hop; hop, hop, hop;
I saw a hungry rabbit *hop*,
   Hop, hop, hop.

He climbed a hill right to the *top*,
   Top, top, top; top, top, top;
He climbed a hill right to the *top*,
   Top, top, top.

He spied a farmer's juicy *crop*,
   Crop, crop, crop …

Ripe carrots he began to *chop*,
   Chop, chop, chop …

23 The hungry rabbit – *photocopiable pictures*

Onset and rime

The angry farmer shouted, *Stop!*
   Stop, stop, stop ...

He aimed his gun and it went *pop,*
   Pop, pop, pop ...

The rabbit let the carrots *drop,*
   Drop, drop, drop ...

As he escaped his ears went *flop,*
   Flop, flop, flop ...

"Next time I'll buy lunch in a *shop,*
   Shop, shop, shop ..."

> Focus -op; sequencing
>
> This is a story song which features onset and rime, and reinforces sequencing. Ask the children to predict some of the *-op* words at the end of each new line.
>
> Play a picture game with the photocopiable illustrations below. Copy them onto separate cards illustrating the story with one *-op* word on each card. Ask the children to sequence them.
>
> Play a word game. Make a set of nine cards on which each of the nine words (*hop, top, crop,* etc.) is written. Can the children sequence these as the song is sung, or match them to the strip of pictures?
>
> Play a different instrument sound with each *-op* word.
>
> | A | B | A | G | E | D | F# | F# |
> |---|---|---|---|---|---|----|----|
> | I | saw | a | hun- | gry | rab- | bit | hop |

24 Old MacGregor's holiday

Tune: Old MacDonald had a farm

Old MacGregor's at the beach, ee i ee i o.
She's throwing pebbles in the sea, ee i ee i o.
   With a *blip-blop* here and a *blip-blop* there,
   Here a *blip*, there a *blop*, everywhere a *blip-blop*,
Old MacGregor's at the beach, ee i ee i o.

Old MacGregor's at the beach, ee i ee i o.
She's going on a donkey ride, ee i ee i o.
   With a *clip-clop* here and a *clip-clop* there,
   Here a *clip*, there a *clop*, everywhere a *clip-clop*,
Old MacGregor's at the beach, ee i ee i o.

… She's watching fish in rocky pools … *flip-flop* …

… She's hoping that it doesn't rain … *plip-plop* …

… She's spreading cream so she won't burn … *slip-slop* …

Onset and rime

Focus: blends featuring l; -ip, -op endings

★ The children can learn this version of the song to experience onset (*bl-*, *cl-*, *fl-*, etc.) and rime (*-ip*, *-op*) and to investigate the consonant blends used in each verse (*bl-*, *cl-*, *fl-*, *pl-*, *sl-* etc.).

G	G	G	D	E	E	D
Old	Mac-	Gre-	gor's	at	the	beach

25 The bat and cat

Tune: The farmer's in the den

Short vowels and CVC words

The *bat* and *cat* are *fat*,
The *bat* and *cat* are *fat*,
   A e i o u,
The *bat* and *cat* are *fat*.

The *pet* I *met* got *wet* ...

The *pin* and *bin* are *tin* ...

The *pot* is *not* so *hot* ...

The *bug* will *tug* the *rug* ...

Long vowels:

He *wakes* and *takes* the *cakes*,
He *wakes* and *takes* the *cakes*,
   A e i o u,
He *wakes* and *takes* the *cakes*.

Onset and rime

Focus	CVC words; short and long vowels

 This simple song develops an awareness of onset and rime. In each verse, the onset changes and the rime stays the same. Sing each verse at a tempo which is comfortable for the children. For the short vowel version, sing *a e i o u* with short vowel sounds, and tap fists together on each letter to accentuate the short sounds.

 Encourage the children to make up more verses of their own, eg
A sad lad feeling bad ...
A red ted in a bed ...
The drum and plum are glum ...

 Sing the long vowel version of the song, with long vowel sounds on *a e i o u*, sliding palms on each letter to accentuate the long sounds. Make up more verses using long vowel sounds, eg
We eat meat for a treat ... The mice and rice are nice ...
I hold the gold she sold ...
The tube is not a cube ...

 Develop the onset and rime to include more complex spelling patterns, eg
See loads of toads on roads ...
A flight at night is right ...

E G	G A	A G
The bat	and cat	are fat

26 Animals' alphabet rap

Rap

Big letters, little letters, alphabet rap,
From A to Z we'll travel without looking at the map!

Big A, little a, bouncing B,
The cat's in the cupboard and she can't see me!

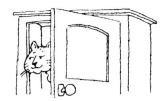

Big D, little d, energetic E,
The frog and the fish are feeding with the flea.

Big G, little g, H, I, J,
The kangaroo and kitten are keen to kick all day.

Big L, little l, M, N, O,
The parrot's pecking pawpaws, spitting all the pips below.

Big Q, little q, R, S, T,
The unicorn's unhappy (he's unreal, you see).

Big V, little v, W X Y,
The zappy zebra zigzags to get her stripes dry.

Big letters, little letters, alphabet beat,
All twenty-six from A to Z and no one had to cheat!

Focus	alliteration; sequencing
	This alphabet rap reinforces the sequence of letters in the alphabet and highlights upper and lower case forms of letters. It also gives the sounds of some of the letters. Introduce it two lines at a time, asking the children to copy you.
	If you wish, you can change the words *Big letters, little letters* in the first and the second last lines of the rap to *Capitals, lower case*.
	Divide the children into two groups to perform alternate lines of the rap.
	Choose children to hold up the letters C, F, K, P, U and Z at the appropriate points in the rap. If you wish, the children can say these letters after each alternate line eg *Big A, little a, bouncing B, **C**!* *The cat's in the cupboard and she can't see me!*
	Add body percussion or an instrumental accompaniment.

Alphabet's tea

Tune: Bobby Shaftoe

A B C D E F G,
All the letters came to tea,
H I J K L M N,
The food was quite delicious.
O P Q R S T U,
V and W, they came too,
X and Y ate all the pie,
And Z washed up the dishes.

 Focus sequence

 Teach or reinforce the sequence of letters in the alphabet with this song.

Using an enlarged photocopy of the alphabet rainbow below, ask a child to point to each letter at the appropriate place in the song. You may like to specify that they follow the lower or upper case alphabet. (By presenting the alphabet in a rainbow shape, all the letters are contained within the visual field.)

F	F	F	B♭	A	C'	A	F
A	B	C	D	E	F	G	__

27 Alphabet Tea – photocopiable alphabet rainbow

28 What shall we do?

Tune: What shall we do with the drunken sailor?

What shall we do with the letter *d*?
What shall we do with the letter *d*?
What shall we do with the letter *d*
On this Monday morning?

Teacher: Let's find words which start with *d*,
All: Let's find words which start with *d*,
Let's find words which start with *d*
On this Monday morning.

Samira: *Desk* and *door* start with *d*,
Thomas: *Ding* and *dong* start with *d*,
Belinda: *Do* and *don't* start with *d*
All: On this Monday morning.

Teacher: Let's find words which end with *d* ...

Lucia: *Send* and *find* end with *d*,
Stephen: *Hand* and *stand* end with *d*,
Edward: *Played* and *stayed* end with *d*
All: On this Monday morning.

Focus finding letters in words

⭐ Choose a letter and ask the children to contribute words to make up new verses for the song. Ask individual children to sing a pair of words beginning (or ending) with the chosen letter.

 Extend the vocabulary of younger children by inventing new verses, eg *Let's find names of farmyard animals ... (or types of transport, different colours).*

 Adapt the song with older children to develop their knowledge of rhyme (*Let's find words which rhyme with Sam*), grammar (*Let's collect some 'doing' words*), letters (*Let's find words which start with vowels*), or syllables (*Let's find words which have two syllables*).

A	A	A	A
What	shall	we	do

Alphabet and letters

Letter shapes

Tune: A-ram-sam-sam

Africa (letter shapes: s m l)

A slinky snake, a slinky snake,

A million monkeys and a slinky snake,

A lion, a lion,

A million monkeys and a slinky snake.

Arctic (letter shapes: e w i)
An eskimo, an eskimo,
A whiskery walrus and an eskimo,
An igloo, an igloo,
A whiskery walrus and an eskimo.

Park (letter shapes: p r s)
A paddling pool, a paddling pool,
A roundabout and a paddling pool,
A seesaw, a seesaw,
A roundabout and a paddling pool.

Focus	writing letter shapes
	Ask the children to draw the shape of the alliterated letter in the air as they sing.
	Think of new verses eg **Toys (b t j)** *A bicycle, a bicycle, Tyrannosaurus rex and a bicycle, A jigsaw, a jigsaw ...* **Pets (c h g)** *A cuddly cat, a cuddly cat, A hairy hamster and a cuddly cat, A gerbil, a gerbil ...*
	Sing a verse as a round in two or three groups, with actions.

C	F	F	F	C	F	F	F
A	slin -	ky snake,	a	slin -	ky	snake	

30 Teatime treats

Tune: Polly put the kettle on

Polly puts the pizza in,
Polly puts the pizza in,
Polly puts the pizza in,
We'll all have tea.

Sukey sizzles sausages,
Sukey sizzles sausages,
Sukey sizzles sausages,
We'll all have tea.

Alphabet and letters

> Focus alliteration
>
> The children can use their own names, and find a food which begins with the same letter or sound to make more verses, eg *Ben bites biscuits bit by bit*; *Carli crunched a carrot cake.*
>
> Notice names which begin with short vowel sounds, eg *Anna* and those which have long vowel sounds, eg *Amy*. Invent your own verses, working through the alphabet, eg
> *Anna asks for apple pie;*
> *Amy aims for apricots.*
>
> | C' | D' | C' | B♭ | A | F | F |
> |----|----|----|----|---|---|---|
> | Pol | - ly | puts | the | piz | - za | in |

31 'Magic e'

Tune: Girls and boys come out to play

'Magic e', oh, 'magic e',
Casting spells so easily,
At to *ate* and *mat* to *mate*,
Wizardry with 'magic e'.

> Focus 'magic e' (split vowel digraph); spelling
>
> Use this song to explore ways of making new words with different vowel sounds by adding 'magic e', eg: *hat* to *hate* and *fat* to *fate*; *tap* to *tape* and *cap* to *cape*; *win* to *wine* and *din* to *dine*; *pip* to *pipe*, and *strip* to *stripe*.
>
> | A | F♯ | G | E | A | F♯ | D |
> |---|----|---|---|---|----|---|
> | 'Ma | - gic | e', | oh, | 'ma | - gic | e' |

32 Bingo lingo

Tune: Bingo

There was a farmer with a dog and *Bingo* was his name-o,
    B – I – N-G-O,
    B – I – N-G-O,
    B – I – N-G-O,
And *Bingo* was his name-o.

There was a goldfish with a son and *Fingo* was his name-o,
    F – I – N-G-O,
    F – I – N-G-O,
    F – I – N-G-O,
And *Fingo* was his name-o.

There was a princess with a dad and *Kingo* was his name-o,
    K – I – N-G-O ...

There was a penguin with a chick and *Pingo* was her name-o ...

There was a pop-star with some drums and *Ringo* was his name-o ...

There was a schoolgirl with a bike and *Tingo* was its name-o ...

There was a robot with a friend and *Zingo* was her name-o ...

Now sing these names along with me
And we'll speak *Bingo Lingo*,
    B – I – N-G-O,
    L – I – N-G-O,
    Bingo, Fingo, Kingo, Pingo,
    Ringo, Tingo, Zingo.

Alphabet and letters

Focus identifying initial phonemes; spelling

 Teach the first verse of the song. Then sing the first line of each of the following verses, omitting the first letter when spelling each name: * – I – N-G-O. Can the children supply the initial consonant and sing it at the appropriate time? (They may need to listen first then add the new letter when the verse is sung a second time.)

 Break down the words into onset and rime: *B–ingo; F–ingo* ...

 Sing each section, spelling the name in two groups:
group 1: *B*, group 2: – *I – N-G-O*.

 Make a set of letter cards with the capital letters *B F K P R T Z*. Can the children choose the matching letter card as each verse is sung? Change the order of verses and mix up the cards for variety.

 Create new verses of the song. Use consonants, eg W – *There was a bird who loved to fly and Wingo was her name-o*; or letter blends, eg St – *There was a wasp who liked to hum and Stingo was her name-o* ...

 Change the short vowel sound in each verse, eg *Bengo, Fengo ... Bango, Fango ... Bongo, Fongo ...*

 Change the final vowel sound, eg *Binga, Finga ... Bingy* (*y* as *-ee*), *Fingy ...*

D	G	G	D	D	E	E	D
There	was	a	far -	mer	with	a	dog

33 Baby's bed

Tune: Goosey, goosey gander

Make a *bed* for baby,
First you need a 'b',
'e' in the middle,
Finish with a 'd'.

Make a *cat* called Curly,
First you need a 'c',
'a' in the middle,
Finish with a 't'.

Make a *dog* called Dozy,
First you need a 'd',
'o' in the middle,
Finish with a 'g'.

Baby's in her *bed* now,
Cat curls on the floor,
As darkness falls, *dog*
Dozes by the door.

Alphabet and letters

 Focus reading and spelling common CVC words

 Sing this lullaby to spell three common CVC words: *bed, cat, dog*.

Show the children how to shape their left fist into a *b* and right fist into a *d*, then place together to make the bed in verse one – a useful reminder when writing these two letters which are often confused.

 On three cards, write the letters *b, e* and *d*. Ask the children to order the cards as they sing verse one. Repeat this activity with *cat* and *dog*.

 Use the photocopiable picture to make all nine letter cards. Give them to pairs or individual children to make each word while singing the song.

C	D	C	E	G		G
Make	a	bed	for	ba	-	by

 e c a t d o g

33 Baby's bed – *photocopiable cards*

34 The wishing well

Tune: Greensleeves

The wishing well is on the hill,
The walls are deep, the waters chill,
The stories tell that it casts a spell,
And makes all of your wishes come true.

Chorus: Drink, traveller, drink your fill,
At the wishing well on the lonely hill.
Drink, traveller, drink your fill,
And may all of your wishes come true.

Word endings

Focus –ll

 After singing the song, ask the children to find all the *-ll* words. Say the words of the song together line by line, writing the *-ll* words down for the children to see.

 Sort the words into three groups: *-all*, *-ell* and *-ill* endings. Stress that while *e* and *i* remain short, *a* yawns when followed by *-ll* (one exception is *shall*).

 Ask the children to make new *-ll* ending words, using the onsets which appear in this song, eg *spell, spill; fill, fall, fell; hill, hall, hell*.

E	G	A	B	C♯	B	A		F♯	D
The	wish	-	ing	well___		is	on	the	hill

Quick, duck, quack

Tune: Heads, shoulders, knees and toes

Quick! Quick, duck, quick, duck, quack,
Quick, duck, quack!
Foxy's coming down the track,
With a sack,
Your friends and you will make a lovely snack.
Quick! Quick, duck, quick, duck, quack,
Quick, duck, quack!

Focus –ck

 This tongue-twister features the *-ck* ending. Sing the song at a slow tempo until the children can articulate the words clearly. Once they have become confident at singing this, they will enjoy trying to get the words right at a faster tempo.

G	A G F# G
Quick!	Quick, duck, quick, duck

36. Huff puff

Tune: The hokey cokey

You do a huff puff here!
A huff puff there!
Huff puff, huff puff,
Little pigs, beware!
I'm a gruff and greedy wolfie,
And I'm ready for my tea,
Here we go, one, two, three!

Chorus: Ooooh, huffy, puffy, puffy!
Ooooh, watch me do my stuffy,
How dare you call me scruffy,
I'll blow your house down, just you see!

Word endings

Focus –ff

- Teach the children this wolf's song from the story of the three pigs, to focus on -*ff* word endings. On the board, write down all the *ff* words in this song and ask the children what they notice about them. (They are all -*uff* endings.)
- Point out to older children the use of the letter -*y* at the end of *huffy, puffy, scruffy* and *stuffy*.

D E	D G	G	G
You do	a huff	puff	here!

37 Party time

Tune: Hickory dickory dock

Jess threw a jelly at Tess!
Bess made a mess on her dress!
Joss got cross, and
Russ made a fuss,
The party was not a success!

> **Focus** –ss
>
> Find the song words ending -ss. Group them into -ess, -oss and -uss endings. Think of more words for each group, eg *chess, less, boss, loss*. (Point out that some words end in the -ss sound but have different spellings, eg *yes, bus*.)
>
> | E | F | G | G | A | B | C' |
> |---|---|---|---|---|---|----|
> | Jess | threw a | | jel | - ly | at | Tess |

38 Sing-song

Tune: My old man's a dustman

Sing, sing, sing a sing-song,
A sing-a sing-song sang,
Sung, sung, sung a sing-song,
A sung-a sing-song sang.

Bing, bing, bing a bing-bong ...

Ding, ding, ding a ding-dong ...

> **Focus** –ng
>
> The onset of the words (*b-, d-,* etc) in this tongue-twister changes in each verse while each of the rimes (*-ing, -ang, -ong, -ung*) remains the same.
>
> When the children know the first verse well, introduce the other verses and ask them to find more onsets to make real and nonsense words, eg
> *ping, ting, wing, swing, pling ...*
> *pong, tong, wong, chong ...*
>
> | F♯ | F♯ | F♯ | | F♯ F♯ | F♯ |
> |----|----|----|----|----|----|
> | Sing, | sing, | sing | | a sing | -song |

Grammar

39 Yes, no

Tune: She'll be coming round the mountain

Leader:	1st group:	2nd group:
Do you like to eat bananas?	Yes, I do.	No, I don't.
Do you like to eat bananas?	Yes, I do.	No, I don't.
Do you like to eat bananas, Like to eat bananas,		
Like to eat bananas?	Yes, I do.	No, I don't.
Can you swim one hundred metres?	Yes, I can.	No, I can't ...
Are you sitting on a pumpkin?	Yes, I am.	No, I'm not ...
Have you ever been to Norway?	Yes, I have.	No, I haven't ...
Will you be at school tomorrow?	Yes, I will.	No, I won't ...

Focus: questions and answers

★ This song introduces the correct forms of answers to common forms of questions. Introduce one question at a time until the children are familiar and confident with the answers. They may all sing the answers together, *Yes, I do*, or they can divide into groups to sing *Yes, I do*, or *No, I don't*, according to choice.

🚀 Ask the children to invent more questions of their own and encourage them to sing them to the class, eg *Can you keep your bedroom tidy? Have you ever swum the Channel?*

🚀 Working in pairs, children can take it in turns to ask questions and to reply to them, eg *Yes, I can* or *No, I haven't*.

C	D	F	F	F	F	D	C
Do	you	like	to	eat	ba	- na	- nas?

40 What's she doing?

Tune: London's burning

Solo:
What's she doing?
That's the question.
Can you guess?
She is reading.

What's he doing?
... He is cooking.

... She is sawing ...

... He is singing ...

... She is laughing ...

All (echo):
What's she doing?
That's the question.
Can you guess?
She is reading.

What's he doing ...
He is cooking.

Grammar

 Focus: questions and answers; verbs

For this song, one child mimes an action without telling the other children what it is. Another child leads the solo and the rest sing the echo. After the third line is sung in solo and in echo, the child who is leading guesses what the mime is to complete the song. Some mimes have been suggested; the children can make up more of their own.

 Point out to older children the use of the question and answer format of the song. Can they say where to put the question marks?

C	C	F		F
What's	she	do	-	ing?

41 This old lady

Tune: This old man

Number one, number one,
Number one is just for fun.
   With a knick knack paddy whack,
   Give the dog a gnome,
This old lady's *jumping* home.

Number two, number two,
Number two has work to do.
   With a knick knack paddy whack,
   Been to see the Dome,
This old lady's *swimming* home.

... Number three grows like a tree ...
... This old lady's *running* home.

... Number four feels sad and sore ...
... This old lady's *sliding* home.

... Number five says, 'Snakes alive' ...
... This old lady's *cycling* home.

Grammar

Focus verbs; number sequence

Begin by chanting the simple fingerplay below. Touch your thumb, then your forefinger and so on, as you say each line:
   Number one – just for fun
   Number two – work to do
   Number three – like a tree
   Number four – sad and sore
   Number five – snakes alive!
Then sing the song.

Sing the song again and ask the children for more 'doing' words to get the lady home. Here are some suggestions: *creeping, skating, stamping, cycling, wobbling, riding, walking*. Discuss all the children's suggestions.

Play a sound on a musical instrument during the last line of each verse. Choose a sound which matches the movement, eg *jumping* – tap wood block; *sliding* – slide a beater over the bars of a xylophone.

Older children can begin to look at spelling rules for adding the suffix *-ing*.

A	F#	A		A	F#	A
Num-ber	one,			num-ber	one	

42 My hat

Tune: My hat, it has three corners

My hat, it is *floppy*,
Too *floppy* is my hat,
Because it is too *floppy*,
I will not wear my hat!

My hat, it is too *spotty*,
Too *spotty* is my hat,
Because it is too *spotty*,
I will not wear my hat!

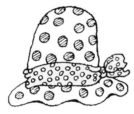

My hat, it is too *stripy*,
Too *stripy* is my hat,
Because it is too *stripy*,
I will not wear my hat!

My hat, it is too *fluffy*,
Too *fluffy* is my hat,
Because it is too *fluffy*,
I will not wear my hat!

Grammar

Focus adjectives

 Sing the song. Ask the children to find more adjectives to explain why they might not like their imaginary hats, eg *woolly, itchy, dirty, muddy, sticky, bobbly, small, big, silly, pretty.* Collect these together and discuss them. Use the children's suggestions to make up new verses for the song.

 The children can design and draw, or paint the hats they have described. Make a hat shop frieze by placing all the designs side by side on shelves, then label them with their descriptions.

 For each verse, choose an instrumental sound to play whenever the adjective is sung (eg maracas for itchy, cymbals for big).

G	C'	G	G	F	E	F	D
My hat,		it	is		too	flop	-py

43 Opposites

Tune: We three Kings of Orient are

Let's all play the opposites game,
Opposites are never the same.
   I say, "Yes,"
   You say, "No,"
Let's all play the game again.

Let's all play the opposites game,
Opposites are never the same.
   I say, "Day,"
   You say, "Night,"
Let's all play the game again.

   ... I say, "Up,"
   You say, "Down," ...

Let's all play the opposites game,
Opposites are never the same.
   I say, "Hot,"
   You say, "Cold,"
Now we've played the opposites game.

Grammar

Focus: antonyms

★ Teach the first two verses to the children. Use the extra verses to ask them to predict the opposite.

🚀 Make more opposite verses. Here are some suggestions:
in, out; near, far; high, low; long, short; fast, slow; happy, sad; fat, thin; young, old; wet, dry; first, last.

🚀 Invite individual children to sing the opposite words: *If I say "push," then Daniel says "pull," ...*

🚀 Change the verb, eg *I shout, cry, yell, whisper, croak, sing ...*

🚀 Show older children the use of speech marks in each verse. Can they write another verse, correctly placing the speech marks?

B	A	G	E	F♯	G	F♯	E
Let's	all	play	the	op-	po-	sites	game

44 What did we read?

Tune: Here we go round the mulberry bush

Teacher:
What did we read at school today,
School today, school today?
What did we read at school today?
Remember, then we'll sing the answer.

(**Meredith:** *We read a story.*)

All:
We read a story at school today,
School today, school today.
We read a story at school today,
We'll read again tomorrow.

(**Eliot:** *We read our names.*)

All:
We read our names at school today ...

Time to go home

Focus	reviewing
	Sing this song at the end of a literacy session or at the end of the school day to remind children of all the reading activities they have been involved with.
	Here are other suggestions of what the children might have read: *some sounds, a poem, a letter, some labels, a big book, letter 'd' words, lots of 'sh' words, a recipe, instructions ...*
	Adapt the song as follows: **Teacher:** *What will you read at school today ...* *Oh, Ali, please tell me your answer.* **Ali:** *I'll read my name at school today ...* *I'll read again tomorrow.*
	You may wish to sing *What did we write?* when this is appropriate.

F	F	F	F		A	C'		A	F
What	did	we	read		at	school		to	- day

Song melodies

1 **Hello around the world** – If you're happy and you know it

3 **Some names** – Pease pudding hot

4 Old MacGregor had a zoo – Old MacDonald had a farm (adapted)
24 Old MacGregor's holiday

6 Chatterbox – Pat-a-cake

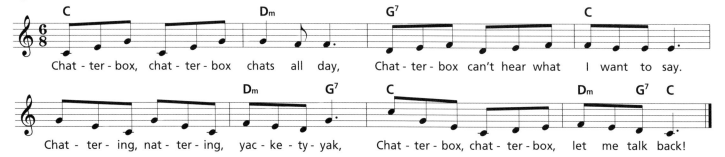

7 My machine – The wheels on the bus

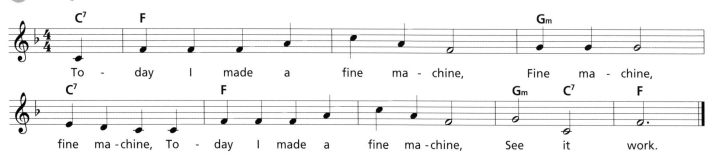

10 **Yoyo** – Oranges and lemons

11 **Grandma and the flea** – A sailor went to sea

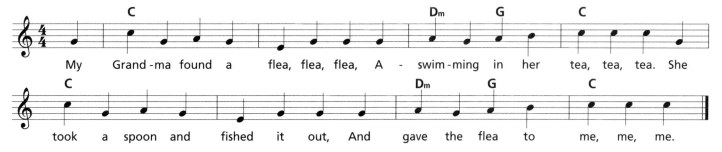

12 Captain of the aeroplane – John Brown's body

15 Hey, little playmate (1st version) – Hush little baby
16 Hey, little playmate (2nd version)

㉑ **Seaside song** – Skip to my Lou

㉒ **Spooky song**

㉓ **The hungry rabbit** – There was a princess long ago

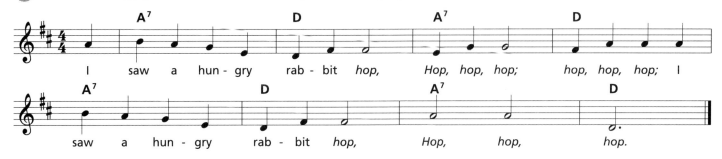

㉔ **Old MacGregor's holiday** – see 4

㉕ **The bat and cat** – The farmer's in the den

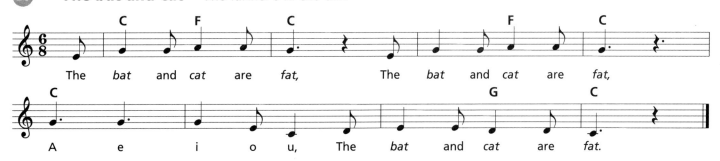

27. Alphabet's tea – Bobby Shaftoe

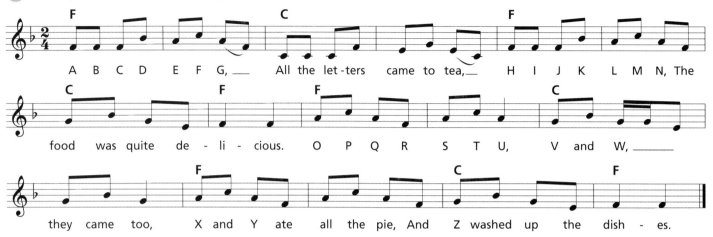

28. What shall we do? – What shall we do with the drunken sailor?

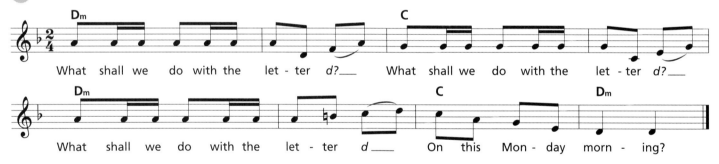

29. Letter shapes – A-ram-sam-sam

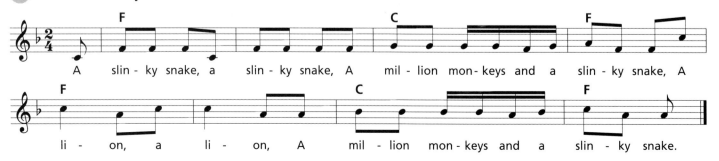

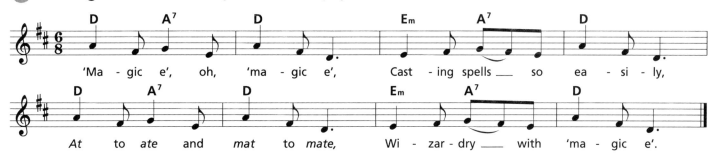

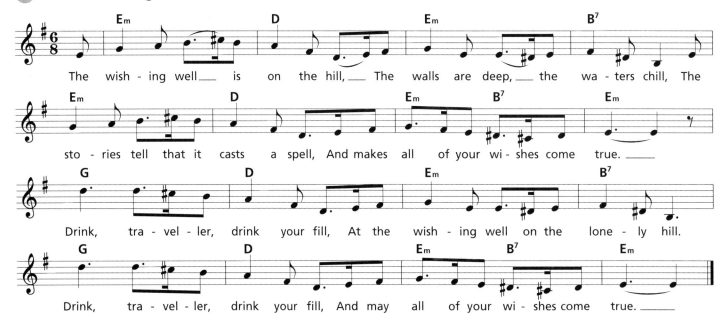

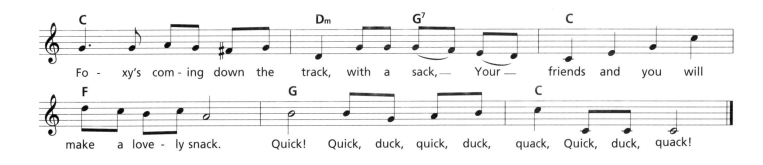

36 Huff, puff – The hokey cokey

37 Party time – Hickory dickory dock

38. Sing-song – My old man's a dustman

Sing, sing, sing a sing-song, A sing - a sing-song sang, Sung, sung, sung a sing-song, A sung- a sing-song sang.

39. Yes, no – She'll be coming round the mountain

L: Do you like to eat ba-na-nas? 1: Yes, I do. 2: No, I don't. L: Do you like to eat ba-na-nas? 1: Yes, I do. 2: No, I don't. L: Do you like to eat ba-na-nas, like to eat ba-na-nas, Like to eat ba-na-nas? 1: Yes, I do. 2: No, I don't.

40. What's she doing? – London's burning

S: What's she do-ing? A: What's she do-ing? S: That's the ques-tion. A: That's the ques-tion. S: Can you guess? A: Can you guess? S: She is read-ing. A: She is read-ing.

41. This old lady – This old man

Num-ber one, num-ber one, Num-ber one is just for fun. With a

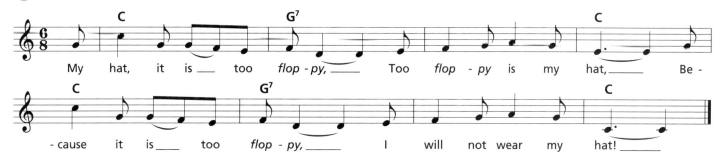

My hat – My hat, it has three corners

Opposites – We three Kings of Orient are

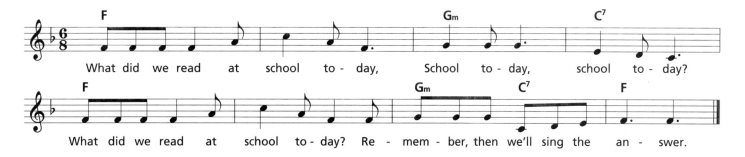

What did we read? – Here we go round the mulberry bush

First lines index

A B C D E F G	27
A peanut sat on the railway track	14
A plate of potatoes, a plate of potatoes	18
A slinky snake, a slinky snake	29
Big letters, little letters, alphabet rap	26
Chatterbox, chatterbox, chats all day	6
Do you like to eat bananas?	39
Giggling baby, hee, hee, hee	21
Hey, little playmate, don't say a thing	16
Hey, little playmate, don't you cry	15
Hush, hush	9
I get in my bed at bedtime	17
I'm captain of the aeroplane and this is my salute	12
I saw a hungry rabbit hop	23
Jamaquack, jamaquack, jamaquack jive	2
Jess threw a jelly at Tess	37
Let's all play the opposites game	43
Let's go for a drive in the little red jeep	19
Let's tell the story of Sleeping Beauty	8
'Magic e', oh, 'magic e'	31
Make a bed for baby	33
My Grandma found a flea, flea, flea	11
My hat, it is too floppy	42
Number one, number one	41
Old MacGregor had a zoo, ee i ee i o	4
Old MacGregor's at the beach, ee i ee i o	24
Once I had a yoyo	10
Owl at midnight, hoo, hoo, hoo	22
Polly puts the pizza in	30
Quick! Quick, duck, quick, duck, quack	35
Scrub-a-dub, scrub-a-dub	5
Sing, sing, sing a sing-song	38
Some names are short	3
The bat and cat are fat	25
The wishing well is on the hill	34
There was a farmer with a dog and Bingo was his name-o	32
Today I made a fine machine	7
What did we read at school today	44
What shall we do with the letter d?	28
What's she doing?	40
When I feel sad I hum a song	20
When you want to say hello around the world	1
Whether the weather is windy	13
You do a huff puff here	36